Hope
the Welcome Fairy

By Daisy Meadows

ORCHARD

www.orchardseriesbooks.co.uk

Fairyland Palace

Hope's House

Troll Hollow

Join

Read the story and collect your fairy points to climb the
Reading Rainbow at the back of the book.

This book is worth 2 stars.

To fairy fans, new and old, who have kept the magic alive.
This is for you.

Special thanks to Rachel
Elliot, Deborah Balogun, Davina
Rungasamy & Jenny Tarr

ORCHARD BOOKS

First published in Great Britain in 2023 by Hodder & Stoughton

1 3 5 7 9 10 8 6 4 2

© 2023 Rainbow Magic Limited.
© 2023 HIT Entertainment Limited.
Illustrations © 2023 Hodder & Stoughton Limited

ISBN 978 1 40836 927 2

Printed and bound in Great Britain by Clays Ltd, Elcograf S.p.A.

The paper and board used in this book are made from wood from responsible sources

Orchard Books
An imprint of Hachette Children's Group
Part of Hodder & Stoughton Limited
Carmelite House, 50 Victoria Embankment, London EC4Y 0DZ

An Hachette UK Company
www.hachette.co.uk
www.hachettechildrens.co.uk

Contents

Story One:
The Glitter Welcome Banner

Story Two:
The Fluffy Teddy Bear

Story Three:
The Sunflower Necklace

Jack Frost's Spell

How dare these trolls invade my home?
They'll wish they'd left Jack Frost alone.
I'll steal some magic from a fairy,
Make their new home super-scary!

How stupid must the troll chief be,
To think that she can mess with me?
I'll treat them all with great disgust,
And turn their village into dust!

Story One
The Glitter
Welcome Banner

Chapter One
A Fresh Start

Leaning out of her bedroom window,
Gracie Adebayo watched the removal van
drive away. She felt a tingle of excitement.
She already loved her new room.

"I hope you like me, Wetherbury," she
whispered. "And I hope I like you!"

Gracie and her mums had moved into

one of the newly built houses in Hawthorn Grove. Everything here was fresh and new, from her bedroom to the park across the street. It was very different from their old flat in the city centre.

Her parents came in carrying more boxes. As usual, her mum looked smart, her black afro curly and shiny. Her mama

had several smears of paint on her face and three pegs in her curly red hair. Gracie grinned at them both.

"I think these boxes are yours," said her mum, placing them on the floor. "There is a lot to unpack."

"I'll start now," said

Gracie eagerly, opening the nearest box. "Oh – paintbrushes."

"Oops, that box should be in my art studio," said her mama.

They went out, and Gracie was about to open a box when something caught her eye.

Through her bedroom window, she could see her next-door neighbours' house. A girl was standing at the window. Her dark brown hair hung in two long plaits, and she was resting her chin on her hands as she stared up at the sky.

Gracie opened her window.

"Hi," she called out.

The girl smiled. "Doesn't the sky look huge?" she said. "In the city there were always buildings between me and the sky. Here, I feel as if I could just grow wings and

fly straight into it."

"I came from a city too," said Gracie.
"I'm Gracie Adebayo."

"I'm Khadijah Khan," said the girl. "I was
hoping that someone my age would live
nearby."

"Same here," said Gracie, smiling.

A stream of brightly coloured bunting
was hanging in Khadijah's window.

"I like your decorations," said Gracie.
"They remind me of ships' flags. Did you
know that sailors use flags to send messages
to other ships?"

Khadijah's eyes sparkled with excitement.

"I've had an idea!" she exclaimed. "I'll
give you some of my bunting, and we can
put messages in our windows."

Gracie felt a rush of happiness. She
hadn't even been here for a full day yet and
she had already made a friend.

"I love that idea," she called across to
Khadijah. "Let's say blue means 'good
morning' and pink means 'good night'."

"Yes!" Khadijah replied happily. "There's
a low fence between our two gardens, so
yellow could mean 'meet me in the garden'.
Let's call it our rainbow signal."

Suddenly, a tiny glowing shape whizzed

between their houses and disappeared into the park opposite. Khadijah gasped and Gracie's heart quickened. There had been something rather unusual about the shape.

"What was that?" Khadijah exclaimed.

"Let's find out," said Gracie. "Come on!"

When Gracie had checked with her

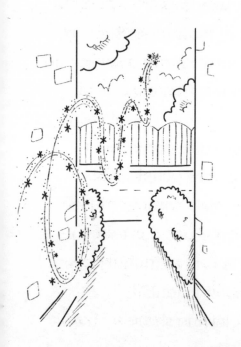

mums and dashed outside, Khadijah was already waiting at her front gate.

"Did your parents say yes?" asked Gracie.

"Not just my parents," said

Khadijah with a smile. "Also my brother Rafi and my grandmother. My grandma's the only one who never tells me what to do."

"It must be fun to have such a big family," said Gracie. "In our house it's just me and my mums."

"Do you like your new house?" Khadijah asked.

"Definitely," said Gracie with a smile. "I'm a bit nervous about starting school, though."

Khadijah gave her a questioning look.

"Every time I meet new people, I have to explain that I was born without my left hand," Gracie told her. "Other children usually ask questions, and it's not always easy to answer them."

"It must be hard," said Khadijah. "But I'll

be with you, so you won't be alone. I have a feeling that we're going to be good friends."

"Me too," said Gracie with a smile.

Chapter Two
New Friends

The girls shared a smile and crossed the road.

"There's going to be a street party here tomorrow," said Khadijah. "Everyone in Wetherbury is coming to meet everyone in Hawthorn Grove."

"Great idea," said Gracie. "I love parties."

"My dad helped to organise it," said Khadijah, pushing open the yellow park gate. "OK, where did that glowing thing land?"

The park was bright and shiny. There was a yellow climbing frame with ladders, rope bridges, a slide and a sliding pole. There was a set of red swings, a green seesaw and a zip line, as well as a trampoline built into the ground, a purple roundabout and a rainbow-coloured climbing wall. A weeping willow stood at the back of the park, surrounded by bushes. Its branches grazed the grass.

The girls checked behind the bushes, around the equipment and even up in the tree. But the glowing shape had vanished.

"Never mind," said Khadijah. "Let's play. Everything looks so much fun!"

Just then, Gracie heard a faint, silvery giggle. She turned, trying to follow the sound.

"What is it?" asked Khadijah.

Gracie shrugged.

"I thought I heard something . . ."

They both listened, but the only sounds were the birds twittering and the leaves rustling in the breeze.

"Want to go on the zip line first?" Khadijah asked.

The girls clambered on together and squealed with excitement as they whizzed along the wire. They bumped to a halt, giggling and breathless.

"Best fun ever!" said Khadijah.

Just then, two older girls walked into the park. The first had wavy blonde hair, and the other's dark hair was straight and to her shoulders. They had matching gold lockets.

"Hi," said the blonde girl. "Isn't this park amazing?"

"Yes, we love it," said Khadijah. "Have you moved to Hawthorn Grove too?"

"No, I'm here visiting my best friend," said the girl. "I'm Rachel Walker and this is Kirsty Tate."

Gracie liked them at once.

"I'm Gracie Adebayo, and this is

Khadijah Khan," she said. "We've just arrived."

"Welcome to Wetherbury," said Kirsty, with a warm smile. "I love it here. Are you going to the street party tomorrow?"

"Definitely," said Khadijah, pulling herself onto the climbing frame. "Come on, let's play!"

The girls clambered over the bars, slid down the pole and competed to see who could climb the highest. Rachel and Kirsty were full of fun, and Gracie forgot about the glowing shape. But as she was running over the rope bridge, she heard another pearl of tinkling laughter.

She stopped, and Khadijah bumped into her. "What was that?"

"I heard it too," said Khadijah, panting.

Gracie saw Rachel and Kirsty share a

quick glance and move towards the bushes.

"Us four are the only people in the park," she whispered, turning to Khadijah.

Khadijah nodded. "Exactly. But where have Rachel and Kirsty gone?"

Gracie whirled around to where she'd seen Rachel and Kirsty moments before.

"They must be in those bushes," she said.

They ran across the rest of the rope bridge and scooted down the slide. As they tiptoed towards the weeping willow, they heard voices among the bushes. First Rachel spoke, then Kirsty. Then a third, higher voice said something.

"Who's that?" Gracie asked, feeling breathless.

Holding hands, they slipped to the back of the park, behind the weeping willow. They peeped out from between

the drooping branches. What they saw made them stare in wonder.

Rachel and Kirsty were kneeling down behind a bush. And there, fluttering in front of them, was a tiny girl with shimmering wings. Gracie and Khadijah gasped.

"I can't believe it," Gracie whispered. "Khadijah, it's a fairy . . ."

Chapter Three
A Magical Surprise

The fairy smiled brightly. Her silky dress was decorated with summer flowers, and her rose-pink sandals shone in the sunlight.

"Welcome to Wetherbury, Gracie and Khadijah," she said. "I'm Hope the Welcome Fairy."

Rachel and Kirsty scrambled to their feet.

"I've always hoped that fairies were real," Khadijah whispered. "But everyone says I should stop dreaming."

"You're not dreaming," said Rachel. "Of course fairies are real."

"We first met them on Rainspell Island," said Kirsty.

"We've had lots of adventures with them and helped to keep their existence secret," said Rachel.

"But now I think it's time that you both know the secret too," said Hope. "There is something special about your friendship with each other and when you befriended Rachel and Kirsty, I knew it was right. I hoped that you would see me."

"Why were you watching us?" asked Khadijah.

"It's my job to watch over children

who are moving to a new home," Hope
explained. "I make sure they settle in well."
Her gauzy wings drooped. "But something
awful happened in Fairyland today."

Rachel and Kirsty looked serious.

"What's happened?" Kirsty asked.

A tall sunflower was nodding its yellow
head by the park fence, and Hope pointed
her wand at it. A stream of golden fairy
dust floated towards the circle of the flower.
At once, a picture appeared.

"It's like looking through a telescope,"
said Khadijah.

They saw a pretty white cottage with
pink flowers all around the windows, and a
green door standing open.

"In my home, friends are always
welcome," said Hope. "I never close my
door to anyone."

29

A crowd of small, green figures tramped into the clean house with muddy, bare feet, shoving each other out of the way. They had bony heads and pointed ears.

"Goblins," said Kirsty, turning to Gracie and Khadijah. "I'm afraid they're often quite naughty."

The goblins were followed by a tall figure dressed all in white. There was frost on his stiff hair and spiky beard. Ice crackled around the doorway as he passed through,

and the pink roses wilted and drooped.

"That's Jack Frost," Rachel explained, shivering. "He's always trying to spoil things for the fairies."

"And there's me," said Hope.

Hope was standing beside a 'Welcome' banner, with a teddy under her arm and a plate of cookies in her hand. She was smiling at the visitors.

"Come in," she began. "Welcome to—"

But before she could finish her sentence, the goblins snatched the cookies and gobbled them up, spraying cookie crumbs all over the floor.

Jack Frost loomed over Hope. He yanked something from around her neck and pulled the teddy from under her arm. The goblins tore down the banner from the wall.

"I will take these," he said coldly.

"Please, stop," said Hope. "I can help you."

"I don't need help from a silly fairy," he sneered.

He strode out, followed by the goblins. The picture in the sunflower vanished.

Khadijah had so many questions that she felt as if she could burst.

"What did he take?" she asked.

"My three most magical objects," Hope explained miserably. "The glitter welcome banner helps people settle into a new home. The fluffy teddy bear makes sure that they can find their way around their new neighbourhood and feel that they belong there, and the sunflower necklace helps them make new friends."

"Oh no," said Rachel, looking worried. "Does that mean as long as Jack Frost has them, no one will be welcoming to newcomers?"

"That's right," said Hope, and her eyes filled with sparkling tears.

"Why has he taken them?" asked Gracie.

"I wish I knew," Hope replied, dabbing her tears away with a sunflower petal. "But when I flew over Wetherbury to find Rachel and Kirsty, I saw goblins lurking in Hawthorn Grove. If I can find them again, maybe they can lead me to my magical objects."

"We'll help you look for them," Khadijah exclaimed. "We'll do whatever we can to help!"

Chapter Four
Goblin Seekers

"We must start right away," said Kirsty. "Let's split up to save time."

"Hope, you should stay with Gracie and Khadijah," said Rachel. "Goblins can be a bit scary, especially if you've never met them before!"

Hope glided over to Gracie and sat on her

shoulder, hidden by her hair. Gracie gasped as the little fairy's wings brushed against her neck. She walked out of the park as smoothly as she could, thrilled that Hope had trusted her so much.

"Hawthorn Grove is built in a big loop," said Khadijah. "If we go one way and you go the other, we'll meet in the middle."

"Good plan," said Rachel. "Good luck, everyone!"

She and Kirsty turned left and headed up the street. Gracie and Khadijah turned right, walking slowly and looking out for goblins.

"I'm tingly with excitement," said Khadijah.

The girls looked behind every bush and wall. They saw a few people unpacking boxes from vans, but there was no sign of green skin or bony heads.

"Look, those boys are going into the show home," said Gracie.

"What's a show home?" whispered Hope from her hiding place.

"It's a house that no one lives in," Gracie explained. "It's there so buyers can see what the new houses look like inside."

A group of boys was going up the path, elbowing and shoving each other. They were all wearing the same white shorts, blue jackets and blue baseball caps. They opened the front door and pushed their way in, all trying to be first.

"Those boys are just as rude as the goblins shoving each other at your house, Hope," said Gracie. "I would have thought they were goblins if they had been as small as you."

"Actually, Jack Frost casts a spell to make goblins grow bigger in the human world," said Hope, thoughtfully. "Those boys really could be goblins!"

Khadijah and Gracie shared a look, their hearts pounding. If they really were goblins, there was no time to go and get Rachel and Kirsty. They might be gone by the time the girls came back. Gracie shivered. Was she really able to stand up to a group of goblins?

"I hope my magic is strong enough," said Hope, and her voice trembled.

Suddenly, Gracie felt braver.

"We can do this together," she said. "Come on. Let's find out what's happened to your things."

Taking a deep breath, the girls stepped through the doorway into the show home.

Loud squawks of laughter were ringing through the house. *Smash! Bang! Crash!* Gracie and Khadijah looked into the sitting room. The "boys" had pulled off their hats and their bony green heads made it clear. These were goblins! They were jumping on the sofas, pulling books off shelves and throwing ornaments at each other.

Suddenly, Hope gasped. "Look at the goblin on the coffee table," she whispered.

He was dancing on the table, kicking up his legs and waving a sparkling lilac-and-green scarf in the air. Or was it a scarf . . . ?

"That's my welcome banner!" Hope exclaimed.

"Stop all that kicking," one of the other goblins grumbled. "You're making me dizzy."

"I'm the one with the banner, so I can do what I like because I'm the best," boasted the dancing goblin.

"Jack Frost didn't give us that to keep," snapped a third goblin. "It was supposed to drive away the trolls. How dare they build a village near the Ice Castle?"

"I don't like trolls," said the first goblin, sitting down on the coffee table. "Will this banner send them away?"

"Nah, it didn't work," said another goblin. "Now we have to hide it from that silly welcome fairy."

A vase whizzed through the air and smashed against the wall.

"They're going to wreck the show home," Khadijah whispered. "We have to think of a plan to stop them – fast!"

Chapter Five
A Royal Welcome

Gracie noticed a CD player on a little table.

"I've got an idea," she said, pressing play. "Conga!"

She danced into the sitting room with Khadijah's hands on her waist.

"CONGA!" yelled the goblins.

They all joined the line, snaking around

the room and out into the hallway. Hope clung on tightly to Gracie as she bounced up and down.

"The one with the banner is right at the back," she stuttered.

Gracie led the dance out of the house and into the street. The goblins squawked with laughter.

"We have to reach the banner," Khadijah panted.

Just then, Rachel and Kirsty came hurrying down the street. This was their chance! Gracie pointed back over her shoulder and led the conga past the older girls. Would they understand?

As the conga passed her, Rachel gently slipped the banner from the goblin's neck. Yes! Gracie and Khadijah broke away. The goblins carried on dancing up the street,

kicking their legs and singing.

Giggling, the girls slipped back into the show home. Rachel handed the banner to Hope, and it shrank to fairy size as soon as she touched it.

"Thank you," she said. "You four make a great team!"

She waved her wand, and instantly the

show home was tidy again.

"Now we must fly," she said. "The king and queen are waiting in Fairyland."

Gracie and Khadijah stared at her, open-mouthed.

"Fairyland?" Khadijah whispered. "Us?"

Hope smiled and tapped each girl lightly with her wand. Glittering, silvery fairy dust sprinkled over them.

"I – I'm shrinking," Gracie exclaimed.

She watched Khadijah, Rachel and Kirsty getting smaller . . . smaller . . . smaller. Then she felt something on her back and looked over her shoulder to see.

"I look like a dragonfly," she whispered.

Khadijah's wings had a pink sheen. She lightly fluttered them and was lifted to her tiptoes. Gracie gave her shoulders a firm wiggle and zoomed upwards.

"Eek!" she cried. "Help!"

Giggling, Rachel and Kirsty swooped after her and led her back to the others.

Hope used her wand to draw a hoop of pure, silver light. Rachel and Kirsty flew through the hoop – and disappeared.

"Your turn," said Hope.

Hand in hand, Gracie and Khadijah flew forwards. A flash of bright light made them squeeze shut their eyes. When they looked again, they were flying above a silver palace with four pink towers. The bluest river they had ever seen shone like a jewel against the green hills.

"Welcome to Fairyland," said Hope, who was flying beside them.

"Wow . . . it's amazing," said Gracie.

Hope led them to the entrance of the palace. They flew down the halls to the room where King Oberon and Queen Titania were sitting on their thrones, wearing glittering crowns and robes of gold and silver.

"Welcome home, Hope," said the Queen with a warm smile. "Welcome back, Rachel and Kirsty. And welcome for the very first time to our newest guests."

"These are our friends, Gracie and Khadijah," said Hope.

She explained how they had helped her save the banner.

"Thank you with all our hearts," said the

King with a small nod.

"You will always find a welcome in Fairyland," the Queen added.

"Please, Your Majesty," said Gracie, feeling very nervous. "Does that mean . . . Are we allowed to come back?"

The Queen looked solemn. "Will you promise to keep the secret of Fairyland, and tell no one about us?"

"We promise," they said together.

"Then we look forward to getting to know you," said Queen Titania.

She held out two shining gold lockets, just like the ones that Rachel and Kirsty were wearing.

"Each locket holds enough fairy dust for one trip to Fairyland," said the Queen. "A pinch will turn you into fairies and back to humans again."

"Thank you," said
Gracie and Khadija,
putting on the lockets.

"And to help you
work together to find
Hope's other missing
objects . . ."

Queen Titania
touched her wand to each of the four
lockets. A stream of sparkling fairy dust
darted between them. For a moment they
were all linked by the silvery light, and then
the glow faded.

"Your lockets are magically connected,"
said the Queen. "Touch them and speak,
and the others will be able to hear you."

Rachel and Kirsty shared a joyful smile.

"Thank you, Your Majesty."

Everyone curtsied. Then Hope hugged

them all goodbye.

"Thank you for helping me today," she said gratefully. "I couldn't have done it without you."

"We're happy to help," said Gracie.

The Queen scattered fairy dust at their feet. It whirled around them, pulling them away.

"Goodbye," they called. "We'll see you soon, Hope, and we won't give up until we find your missing objects!"

Story Two
The Fluffy Teddy Bear

Chapter Six
Lost and Confused

Khadijah woke up to the sound of birds singing. Smiling, she jumped out of bed and opened her window. Gracie's curtains were already open, and a yellow flag was hanging there.

"That means 'meet me in the garden'," Khadijah remembered.

She got dressed and ate breakfast quickly, feeling excited. She could hardly believe that they had met fairies the day before. When she ran out to the low fence between their gardens, Gracie was already there, jumping up and down with excitement.

"Did it really happen or did I dream it?" she burst out.

Khadijah laughed. "I was thinking the same thing," she said. "But it did happen." She looked around and lowered her voice. "We met real fairies and went to Fairyland with Rachel and Kirsty."

"I'm so glad it wasn't a dream," said Gracie, smiling. "I can't wait to see Hope again."

"Same here," said Khadijah. "After all, the fluffy teddy bear and the sunflower necklace are still missing."

"Until she visits us again, how about exploring Hawthorn Grove?" said Gracie.

"Great idea," Khadijah agreed. "I want to get to know every nook and cranny."

"Let's go straight away," suggested Gracie. "I'll meet you at the front."

Khadijah ran back inside, where her mum told her to be back in time for lunch. The girls met on the pavement outside their houses.

"Let's start at the park," Khadijah suggested.

"Great idea," said Gracie. "It's really

close and we didn't get to see it all yesterday."

"Yes," said Khadijah, frowning. "I remember . . . it only took a few seconds to get there."

"Did we go left or right?" Gracie asked.

They stared at each other, trying to remember.

"This is strange," said Khadijah. "I know it's nearby, but I can't think where."

Just then, they heard someone calling their names. On the other side of the street,

their new friends Rachel and Kirsty were waving from the yellow park gate.

"Of course," Khadijah exclaimed. "The park is opposite our houses. How could we have forgotten that?"

They crossed the road. When they reached the other side, Gracie looked back over her shoulder.

"Khadijah, I can't remember which house is mine," she said in alarm.

Rachel held open the park gate, and Kirsty gave Gracie a hug.

"Try not to worry," she said. "You're forgetting because Jack Frost still has the fluffy teddy bear. It helps people to find their way around their new neighbourhood, and to feel that they belong. Without it, anyone who has just moved house will be confused."

Khadijah felt better at once.

"Let's not worry about Jack Frost," said Rachel. "Queen Titania always says that you have to wait for the magic to come to you. So in the meantime, let's play!"

The park soon filled up with village children and newcomers from Hawthorn Grove. Everyone was friendly and playing together. Shouts of laughter filled the air. It was so much fun that Khadijah got a shock when she checked her watch.

"It's nearly lunchtime," she said in surprise. "That went quickly!"

After a final spin on the roundabout, the four girls jumped off, giggling and feeling dizzy. Most of the others had already left. A few Hawthorn Grove children were still outside the park gate.

"They look upset," said Rachel in a

worried voice. "I wonder what's wrong."

"I can guess," said Gracie. "They must have forgotten how to get back to their new homes!"

Chapter Seven
Special Delivery to Fairyland

The Hawthorn Grove children were
trembling. Kirsty and Rachel smiled kindly
at them.

"Have you forgotten where you live?"
Rachel asked.

"Not exactly," said one girl miserably.
"We can all remember our addresses. We

just can't remember how to get there."

"We'll help," said Kirsty. "If we keep going, we'll pass everyone's house. Follow us."

They led the way around the loop, reading out the number of each house they passed. One by one, the lost children found their homes. When only Gracie and Khadijah were left, they were almost back at the park. They walked past a red postbox.

"That's so bright and shiny," said Gracie. "It almost looks as if it's glowing."

Khadijah heard a faint tinkling sound and pressed her ear against the side of the postbox.

"I think there's something inside," she said in astonishment.

With a silvery laugh, Hope came

whizzing out of the letter slot. She zoomed around them and then landed on Gracie's little arm as lightly as a butterfly. The others huddled around her so that no one would see.

"I have found out what Jack Frost has done with my fluffy teddy bear," she exclaimed. "Will you come to Fairyland with me?"

Khadijah and Gracie shared an excited smile and nodded. They could hardly wait to see Fairyland again.

The girls crouched behind the postbox, and Hope waved her wand. They were showered in sparkling fairy dust, and Khadijah felt herself shrinking. The postbox suddenly looked as big as a skyscraper!

"Hooray!" Gracie exclaimed. "We're

fairies again!"

Khadijah fluttered her delicate wings and felt herself leave the ground.

"Come on," said Hope. "Time to post ourselves to Fairyland."

She flew into the letter slot with

Rachel and Kirsty right behind her. Gracie
and Khadijah reached for each other's
hand and flew after them.

For a moment, everything went black.
Then the blackness faded to a dull grey
light. They landed with a bump on
something hard.

"Cobblestones," said Gracie.

They were standing on a cobbled path
that led to an old humpbacked bridge. It
crossed a fast-flowing river. There was no
snow, but it was bitterly cold.

"*Brr*, it's freezing here," said Gracie.
"There are lumps of ice in the water."

"We must be close to Jack Frost's Castle,"
said Rachel.

"Yes," Kirsty agreed. "Goblin Grotto is
not far from here."

"This is where the trolls have built their

new home," said Hope.

She pointed to a roughly painted sign on the other side of the bridge:

Troll Hollow
You Are NOT Welcome

Beyond the sign, a winding path led towards the village. Several other signs had been hammered into the ground.

Go Away
Trespassers Will Be Gobbled Up
No Goats Allowed

"It isn't as cosy and welcoming as Hawthorn Grove," said Gracie.

"The trolls don't mind the cold because their skin is so thick," Hope said. "And they are definitely not welcoming."

She pointed to the bridge and the fairies

gasped. A teddy bear had been tied to the middle of the bridge. Its head was drooping sadly and its fur was scruffy.

"Is that your teddy?" Khadijah asked Hope.

Hope nodded. "Jack Frost tied it there. He thought it would send the trolls back to their old home, but he doesn't understand how my magic works. He has made the trolls feel at home here."

Khadijah looked around. There was no sign of Jack Frost or the trolls.

"Time to rescue the teddy!" she exclaimed.

She rose into the air and zoomed towards the bridge.

"Wait!" Kirsty called out. "It could be a trap!"

But Gracie was by Khadijah's side.

"It'll be all right," she said. "We can do anything!"

But as soon as they landed, there was a terrible roar from below.

"Who's that tip-tapping over my bridge?"

The ground shook. Something huge was coming.

Chapter Eight
Under the Bridge

A massive figure lumbered out from underneath the bridge. She had lumpy, bumpy, purple-grey skin. Her glaring eyes were yellow, and her nose looked round and swollen. Horns rose up over huge, flappy ears and a clump of thick, tangled hair. Gracie clutched at Khadijah. "I think it's a

troll," she whispered.

"You think right!" exclaimed the troll.

In one quick movement, she sprang up on to the bridge, and snatched the teddy. Khadijah and Gracie stumbled backwards.

Khadijah's voice shook as she spoke. "Please, that teddy belongs to our friend Hope."

The troll's eyes narrowed. "So?"

"People in the human world can't settle in to their new homes without it," said Gracie.

"Do you know what that is?" the troll asked. "NOT MY PROBLEM!"

Chuckling at her own rudeness, she ambled away from them towards Troll Hollow.

"A prize like this should be in the main square," they heard her muttering.

Khadijah and Gracie felt awful.

"We should have waited," cried Gracie.

Rachel, Kirsty and Hope fluttered on to the bridge beside them.

"We're sorry," added Khadijah.

Hope put her arms around them both.

"It's OK," she said. "We know where the teddy has gone."

A noise made them turn around. Khadijah gasped. Jack Frost was striding towards the bridge, dragging three cowering goblins. Ice crackled over the cobbles as he drew nearer. His white cloak

clinked with icicles.

"You scaredy-cats will go on to the bridge and get my teddy," he was yelling at the goblins. "I need its magic for a new plan."

He was so busy shouting that he didn't notice the fairies until he had reached the bridge. Then he stopped and scowled at them.

"What are you doing here?" he demanded. "And where's my bear?"

"It's Hope's bear," said Rachel, firmly. "And it's been taken to the troll village."

"We're here to rescue it," Kirsty added bravely.

Jack Frost spun around to face his goblins. They staggered backwards.

"Go and get that bear," he hissed, jabbing his bony finger at them.

"P-please don't make us," wailed the goblins. "Trolls are scary."

"We have to go in to the village," Kirsty whispered to the others. "It's our only chance to find the bear."

Khadijah shivered. She didn't like the idea of meeting more trolls!

The goblins were still wailing as the fairies flew over the bridge and followed the winding path to Troll Hollow. They saw more unwelcoming signs on the way.

Leave Now
Turn Back

Clear Off
Trespassers Make Yummy Snacks

They landed in a wide cobbled street. It was lined with low houses made of boulders. The roofs were shaped like bridges, making each home look like a cave.

"Let's see how trolls live," said Gracie daringly.

The fairies tiptoed closer and peeped through a window.
They saw no
furniture. Instead,
a troll family
was lying back
on cushions and
beanbags, sharing
cookies shaped like
goblins. A young
troll rammed three

cookies into his mouth at once.

"Manners!" rasped his mother. "You can fit more than that in."

"Goodness, I think they might be even messier than goblins," whispered Kirsty, pointing to the dirty plates and goblets on the troll family's floor.

"We have to find the main square," said Hope. "That's where the troll was taking the teddy."

The fairies tiptoed on. At the end of the street, they reached a large square. There was a café, and outside it were a few stone picnic tables. A large statue of a proud-looking troll was standing in the middle. It had one foot resting on the backs of three goats.

Hope gave a squeak of excitement. "My teddy!"

Her magical bear had been tied to one of the the horns of the largest goat. They looked around but there were no trolls in sight.

"Maybe they're all busy eating," said Gracie in a low voice.

"I'm just glad they're not here," Khadijah replied. "Shall

we go and get the bear?"

She saw Rachel and Kirsty exchange a glance.

"OK," said Kirsty. "It's now or never!"

Chapter Nine
Troll Feast

Khadijah's heart was thumping hard as they landed by the statue. She noticed a shiny brass plaque below it.

Never Trust a Goat.

"Trolls are afraid of goats," Hope explained. "Something to do with the Billy

Goats Gruff family."

Their fingers trembled as they worked at the tight knots.

"Oh no," said Gracie. "No one is on lookout."

"Too late!" shouted a voice behind them.

A net dropped on their heads. It crumpled their wings and knocked them to the ground. They heard a mean chortle and saw a group of trolls grinning at their own

cleverness. The biggest troll waggled her thick fingers at them.

"Got you," she said, showing higgledy-piggledy brown teeth. "Chumps."

Each fairy was pulled out of the net and yanked to her feet.

"Hold their arms behind them," the biggest troll ordered. "Stop them from using their wings or their wands."

"Yes, chief," said the trolls.

The trolls marched the five fairies back to the bridge. On the way, troll families came to their windows and doors, staring and jeering.

"How are we going to escape?" asked Gracie.

Kirsty glanced at Hope. "Can you use your wand?"

Hope shook her head. "She's holding my

arms too tightly. I can't wave my wand at all."

When they reached the bridge, Jack Frost was still arguing with his goblins.

"Go away!" he shouted as soon as he saw the trolls. "Find somewhere else to build a village."

The chief troll clumped on to the bridge, and Jack Frost met her halfway. He folded his arms and glared at her.

"You sent these spindly fairies to steal our bear," she growled.

"My bear," Jack Frost snapped back.
"And I would never work with the fairies!
I work against them. I love spoiling their
fun."

The chief troll raised her bushy eyebrows.

"Me too," she said. "They are puny and
annoying. What do you call a fairy who
needs a bath? Stinkerbell!"

Jack Frost cackled with laughter. "Why
do fairies like toadstool houses? Because
there's not mush-room inside!"

Jack Frost threw back his head and

laughed. The chief troll wiped tears of laughter from her eyes.

"They're getting on well," said Khadijah in surprise.

"You're right," Hope said, excitedly. "And if they are focusing on each other, we might be able to slip away."

"The more they dislike us, the more they like each other," said Kirsty.

"So we have to annoy them," said Rachel thoughtfully. "Hey, Jack Frost! Chief troll! Goodness and kindness will always win over your mean tricks."

The chief troll rolled her eyes.

"They're almost as pesky as goats," she grumbled.

"I would love to see them lose," said Jack Frost, longingly. "Just once."

"Me too," said the chief. "But they always

seem to come out on top."

"If only my goblins weren't such scaredy cats," Jack Frost said, curling his lip. "I've nearly beaten the fairies lots of times."

The troll chief patted him comfortingly on the back. Jack Frost staggered sideways.

"I'd like to hear your stories," she said. "Join us for refreshments."

She clicked her fingers. A few moments later, trolls appeared with trays of food and drink.

"Sit down," the chief said. "Bilberry cordial? Goat-hair cookies? Boulder cakes?"

Soon, almost all the trolls were lying down, gobbling snacks. Bilberry cordial was running down their chins. Jack Frost had perched stiffly on a boulder and was telling the trolls about the time he had nearly defeated Samira the Superhero Fairy. His goblin servants were lingering near the fairies, their knees knocking together.

The only trolls not lying down were the ones holding the fairies. As they watched their friends feasting, their tummies began to rumble. It sounded like far-off thunder. The goblins edged away nervously.

"I can't stand this any more," said the troll holding Kirsty.

"Me neither," said the one holding Gracie. "Those greedy guts won't leave any for us."

"The chief told us not to let the fairies go," said the smallest troll, who was holding Khadijah.

"Pah," said the first troll in a scoffing voice. "They're so spindly and weak that they're bound to be cowards. They're too scared to move."

"I've got an idea," whispered Gracie's

troll. "Let's pretend that we eat fairies." She turned to Gracie and pulled a horrible face. "Listen, you stay behind this boulder or we will turn you into fairy cakes and gobble you up!"

The fairies nodded, pretending to look frightened. Grinning, the trolls pushed them to the ground and ambled towards the food.

"We have to fly upwards as soon as they are out of sight," said Hope in an urgent whisper. "One . . . two . . . three . . . FLY!"

Chapter Ten
Home Sweet Home

WHOOSH! The five fairies zoomed into the air. A cry went up from the crowd of trolls.

"We've been seen!" cried Rachel. "Fly as fast as you can!"

They all made a beeline for the main square. The trolls were thundering along below, but the fairies were faster. They reached the main square and dived towards the teddy. There were just three more knots to undo.

"Stop them!"

The angry shouts and pounding feet sounded very close. Two knots to go.

"You interfering fairies!"

The chief burst into the main square with Jack Frost and charged towards the statue. One more knot left . . .

"YES!" Khadijah shouted.

She and the other fairies flew up into the grey sky with the teddy bear. Below, the chief was yelling at the trolls who had let the fairies go.

"How can I ever thank you?" said Hope, hovering in the air. "Without you, the trolls would have kept my bear here for ever."

"You don't need to thank us," said

Khadijah, laughing. "We love helping."

"Just promise that you'll let us help again," Gracie added, her eyes sparkling.

"I promise," said Hope.

She raised her wand, and the grey clouds seemed to wrap around them like blankets. It felt like sinking into the squashiest, comfiest chair in the world. Khadijah's eyelids drooped . . .

. . . And suddenly they were standing outside their houses in Hawthorn Grove.

"Do you recognise them now?" asked Rachel with a smile.

"Yes," said Gracie, laughing. "The rainbow signals in our bedroom windows make them feel like home."

"What an amazing morning!" said Khadijah.

One by one, they all linked arms.

"Let's always remember our promise to keep the fairies secret," Kirsty said.

"And fingers crossed we see Hope again very soon," said Khadijah.

"I can't wait to meet all our new neighbours at the party," said Gracie. "After everything that has happened this morning, I am really starting to feel that I belong here!"

Story Three
The Sunflower Necklace

Chapter Eleven
A Suspicious Start

Khadijah's kitchen was filled with
people, chatter and yummy smells. The
street party was starting outside. Her
grandmother, her father and her brother
Rafi had been cooking all day. They
had made some of Khadijah's favourite
foods, including samosas, stuffed parathas

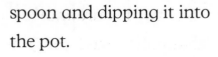

and masala dosa to share with their new neighbours.

"I'll do some tasting," Khadijah's grandmother said, picking up a big wooden spoon and dipping it into the pot.

Khadijah watched her grandmother's tasting spoon dip in and out of the dal and smiled. It was a familiar sight.

"More salt," her grandmother murmured, moving to the next pot. "Hmm, just right . . . add more chilli . . . good . . ."

Smiling, Khadijah dashed outside. Gracie was already in the street, helping her mums to drape white cloths over the long line of tables down the centre of the road. Jewel-coloured bunting fluttered in the breeze.

"Hi," said Gracie, smiling. "Isn't this amazing? No cars allowed. We can dance in the street!"

She twirled around, laughing. Everywhere Khadijah looked, something exciting was happening. Musicians were tuning their guitars, ukuleles and fiddles. One of their neighbours was setting up steel drums. There was even a lady with a harp. Barbecues were sizzling and delicious smells filled the air. Lots of people from the village had arrived and were chatting to each other.

"Come and meet my mums," said Gracie. Her mum gave Khadijah a big smile.

"I'm Chioma," she said. "This is my wife, Michelle. I hope you like Nigerian food!"

She showed Khadijah the dishes they

were putting on the tables.

"Jollof rice, pounded yam and efro riro, moi moi and coconut candy," said Michelle.

Khadijah's mouth was watering. "I can't wait to try everything!"

Someone called her name. Rachel and Kirsty were hurrying down the street with Kirsty's parents. They were all carrying bowls of food. Gracie introduced her mums.

"This is a great chance to make new friends," said Michelle with a smile.

"I quite agree," said Mr Tate. "It's lovely to have new neighbours."

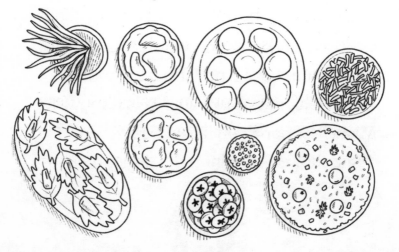

Khadijah looked around.

"I think we're the only ones," she said.

No one else from the village was chatting to the Hawthorn Grove newcomers.

"Perhaps they'll relax when they're eating," said Chioma. "Food and music normally get people talking."

Gracie spoke quietly to the other girls. "Everyone looks awkward and suspicious of each other."

"It's because Hope's sunflower necklace is missing," said Kirsty. "People in Wetherbury are usually really friendly."

"They won't be able to make new friends until Hope has her necklace back," said Rachel.

THUNK! An empty bowl rolled off the nearest table. Gracie went to pick it up, but as she reached it, the bowl rolled under the

table. Gracie ducked under the tablecloth.
The bowl had landed upside down. Gracie
picked it up . . . and out fluttered Hope!

Chapter Twelve
Fairy-Napped!

Feeling excited, Gracie pushed her head under the tablecloth and beckoned to the others.

Khadijah, Rachel and Kirsty quickly joined her.

"We're so glad you're here, Hope," Kirsty added breathlessly. "Without your sunflower necklace, no one is making friends."

Hope nodded. "Everyone feels safe with things they're used to," she said. "It takes courage to taste new food, meet new people or try new things. That's why my sunflower necklace is so important. Without it, no one is brave enough to make new friends."

Loud shouts in the street made them all jump.

Hope gasped. "What was that?"

Khadijah opened her pocket and Hope tucked herself inside. Then all four girls crawled out from underneath the tablecloth. They soon saw that it was just one family making all the noise. The father was standing with his back to the girls, and his sons were jumping over the tables, yelling at each other and having pretend

battles with the chairs.

"Be careful of the food!" called Chioma.

One of the boys stomped in a bowl of curry and shrieked. Chioma shook her head and went to speak to the father.

The boy sat down on the table and started licking his foot.

"Wow, he has big feet for such a small boy," said Khadijah.

"Very big," said Rachel in a worried voice. "I think he's a goblin!"

Kirsty put her hand over her mouth. "So his dad must be . . ."

The girls stared as Chioma tapped the man on the shoulder. He turned around. He had spiky white hair, and his beard looked like icicles.

"Jack Frost!" Khadijah cried out.

"What is he doing here in Hawthorn Grove?" asked Kirsty.

"He's sure to be up to mischief," Rachel replied. "And look – he's wearing the sunflower necklace!"

Just then, Jack Frost saw the girls and his ice-cold eyes narrowed.

"He's coming straight towards us," said Gracie with a squeak of alarm.

The four girls darted out of sight around

the corner. Seconds later, Jack Frost came striding after them. His breath misted the air, and the ground under his feet crackled with ice. The girls pressed themselves against the wall.

"Where is she?" he snapped.

Khadijah felt Hope tremble in her pocket.

"W-we w-won't t-tell you," she said, bravely.

"I only want to talk to her," snarled the Ice Lord. "Or is she a cowardy custard?"

Khadijah felt her pocket move, and then

Hope's head peeped out.

"I'm not a coward," she said in a calm voice.

Jack Frost pointed one long, bony finger at her.

"Tell me how to make the necklace work," he demanded. "I used it to throw an unwelcome party for the trolls, but everything came out wrong. The trolls are having a good time."

"But you were getting on with the trolls when we left Fairyland," Rachel blurted out. "Why do you want to upset them?"

Jack Frost curled his thin lips.

"That troll chief keeps trying to boss me around," he muttered. "But this stupid necklace won't even let me be rude to her."

"My necklace could never make anyone feel unwelcome," said Hope gently. "The magic doesn't work like that."

Jack Frost's eyes blazed. He pointed his finger at Hope.

"I want that necklace to make the trolls feel unwelcome," he yelled. "And you will be my prisoner until you tell me how!"

There was a dazzling flash of blue lightning. The girls closed their eyes. When they looked again, Jack Frost had vanished . . . and so had Hope.

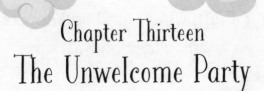

Chapter Thirteen
The Unwelcome Party

Khadijah and Gracie shared a horrified look.

"What are we going to do?" asked Gracie.

Rachel and Kirsty were already opening their lockets. Of course! Each of them had been given enough fairy dust for a trip to Fairyland. Quickly, they sprinkled the sparkling powder over their heads.

"Oh, how pretty," said Gracie, looking up.

A tiny, fluffy white cloud had appeared just above them, glittering with silver sparkles.

The cloud grew bigger, surrounding them in a dazzling white mist and in a few seconds they were fairy size. Feather-light

wings fluttered on their backs.

"Concentrate on the Ice Castle," said
Kirsty. "He's probably taken Hope there."

Khadijah closed her eyes and pictured
Jack Frost's home. She felt herself
whooshing away from Hawthorn Grove.
Her skin tingled with cold, and then she
was standing with her friends in the garden
of the Ice Castle. A shiver ran down her
spine.

"It's so grim
and grey," Gracie
whispered.

"It's even worse
inside," Kirsty
told her. "And it is
always guarded by
goblins."

"We have to

work out a way to get in," said Rachel.

Khadijah noticed that the castle was on a hill. Below, she could see a collection of huts.

"Is that where the goblins live?" she asked.

"Yes, that's Goblin Grotto," said Kirsty. "It's—"

A rowdy cheer interrupted them.

"A toast to Jack Frost and his amazing party!"

The fairies exchanged a glance and then zoomed around to the back of the castle. The troll chief was standing in the frost-covered garden. She was holding up a goblet of bilberry cordial. Jack Frost was facing her, scowling. A crowd of trolls was gathered around them, together with many sulky-looking goblins.

"After our old home was destroyed by a

storm . . ." she began.

"Sent by Jack Frost," one of the trolls
called out.

There was a roar of laughter and Jack
Frost's scowl deepened. The chief grinned.

". . . We travelled a long way to find the
perfect spot for our new village," she went
on. "We built Troll Hollow as close as we
could to this castle, just to annoy you. We

were planning to make you pay to cross the bridge." She chuckled at Jack Frost. "But I've found out that we've got a lot in common. We love food, and we can't stand those goody-two-shoes fairies. You've even thrown us a party!"

One of the trolls glanced around, and the fairies ducked behind a bush. Jack Frost was starting to look less annoyed. The chief got closer, until her round nose was touching his sharp one.

"I've had an idea," she said with a toothy smile. "If you let us live in Troll Hollow, I'll lend you trolls to help you defeat the fairies."

"That's our job!" shouted a grumpy-looking goblin.

"Only when your goblins can't cope," the chief added.

Jack Frost rubbed his hands together.

"It might work," he said.

Khadijah and Gracie glanced at Rachel and Kirsty.

"This doesn't sound good," said Khadijah.

The chief and Jack Frost clinked goblets and drank.

"Now, what shall I do with that silly Welcome Fairy?" Jack Frost asked.

"Keep her locked up," the chief said, shrugging.

"I suppose having a fairy prisoner might be useful," said Jack Frost. "Fine, she can stay in Goblin Grotto."

"No!" exclaimed Rachel.

She burst out from their hiding place,
followed by Kirsty.

"You can't keep Hope prisoner," Kirsty
exclaimed.

"I don't need a fairy's advice," Jack Frost
yelled. "And I don't need this."

He pulled the necklace off his neck and
dropped it on the ground.

Rachel and Kirsty dived for it, and Jack
Frost jabbed his wand at them. There was
a blue flash . . . Rachel was holding the
necklace but she and Kirsty were frozen
solid.

Chapter Fourteen
Rescue Mission

"We have to go!" cried Gracie. "We can't fight Jack Frost, trolls and goblins!"

She pulled Khadijah into the air and they zoomed away from the castle. It felt awful to have left their friends behind.

"What are we going to do?" Gracie asked.

"There's only one thing we can do," said

Khadijah. "We have to fly to Goblin Grotto and try to rescue Hope."

Their hearts thumping with fear, the fairies flew towards the lights of Goblin Grotto. Soon they were fluttering down into a narrow, empty street. Their feet sank into thick snow.

"Where is everybody?" asked Gracie.

They tiptoed past many small wooden huts. Khadijah peeped through a few windows.

"No one's home," she said eventually. "Maybe they're all at the unwelcome party."

"But where is Hope?" asked Gracie.

The main square was deserted too. The fairies felt helpless. They had no idea where to look or what to do. But then . . .

"Listen," said Khadijah.

A sad, silvery voice was singing somewhere nearby.

"Open the door, stoke up the fire,
New friends will soon be here.
Sing cheery songs, smile in delight,
Welcome, welcome, my dear."

The voice broke, and they heard a little sob.

"That's Hope!" Gracie whispered. "Come on."

The song began again. They followed the sound along a little alleyway. At last they saw a hut with smoke curling out of the chimney.

"It's coming from in there," said Khadijah.

They peeped through the window and gasped. Hope had been tied to a chair in the middle of the room. Behind her, in the tiny kitchen, two goblins were stirring something in a bowl.

"That's too much salt for bogmallows," they heard the taller goblin squawk.

"Just add more bog juice," the shorter goblin retorted. "Stop grumbling."

"It's that awful singing," said the first goblin. "She's giving me a headache."

Gracie and Khadijah ducked as the goblins turned and glared at Hope.

"Shut up!" they yelled together.

Gracie eased open the door. She and Khadijah slipped inside.

Hope saw them at once, and happiness sprang into her eyes. They gestured to her to keep singing as they looked around.

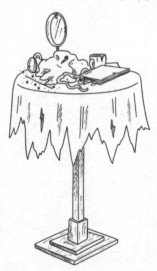

Was there anything they could use to free the little fairy? The only table was covered with dirty cups, an old mirror, hair ribbons, torn clothes, ripped books . . . and Hope's wand.

The girls shared a joyful

– and silent – high five. As soon as they untied Hope, she would be able to use her magic to escape.

The goblins were squabbling about how much mildew they needed. It was now or never! With trembling fingers, Gracie and Khadijah picked at the knots.

"We have to hurry," Khadijah whispered.

"Rachel and Kirsty got your necklace, but Jack Frost froze them," Gracie added, panting. "Oh dear, these knots are tough."

They glanced at the goblins, willing them not to turn around. Finally, the last knot loosened.

"Yes!" whispered Hope.

She pulled her hands free and rubbed her wrists. Then she picked up her wand.

CRACK!

Blue lightning streaked across the room, and the fairies fell back. Jack Frost was standing in the doorway.

"Now I've got you," he raged, raising his wand. "I'll freeze you all!"

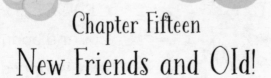

Chapter Fifteen
New Friends and Old!

Khadijah snatched the old mirror from the table. She held it up just as the freezing spell shot towards them. The spell bounced off the glass and back at Jack Frost.

"NOOO!" he shouted.

With a chilling crackle, ice enveloped his feet and crept up his legs. *CRACKLE!*

His cloak was stiff with frost. *CRACKLE!* His legs and body were wrapped in ice. *CRACKLE!* His arms . . . his neck . . . he opened his mouth to yell, but no sound came out.

He was frozen to the spot, his mouth still wide open.

"Yes!" cried Gracie, jumping up and down with a cheer.

The goblins clutched each other and wailed in shock.

"He will soon defrost," Hope told them. "Ice can't hold Jack Frost for long."

The goblins shared a look of panic.

"I don't want to be here when he thaws out," said the taller one. "Let's go to the party and see if there's any food left!"

"That's where we need to go too," said Khadijah as the goblins left.

Even though Jack Frost couldn't move, it was scary to edge past him and out of the hut.

"I hope the ice holds him long enough for us to reach the others," Hope panted as they flew away.

The unwelcome party had moved away from the garden to the front of the castle. But a large, grumpy-looking troll was guarding the frozen fairies.

"Oh no," said Khadijah with a groan.

They hid behind a statue of Jack Frost, their hearts sinking. The troll was sitting with her back against a bush, her arms folded. Hope's eyes filled with tears.

"I can't get to them," she said. "She'll grab us as soon as she sees us."

"Maybe not," said Gracie, her eyes suddenly sparkling. "I've had an idea. Hope, could you make me sound like a troll?"

Hope looked puzzled but nodded and tapped Gracie with her wand. Gracie fluttered into a tree and cupped her hand around her mouth.

"The food's almost gone," she called in a gravelly troll voice. "Only a few boulder cakes left. Yummy!"

The troll guard scrambled to her feet.

"It's daft guarding these fairy icicles," she muttered to herself. "I'm not missing out on my grub!"

She lumbered away. Immediately, Hope

darted forwards and tapped Rachel and Kirsty with her wand. The ice turned to water, and they were free. Gracie and Khadijah hugged them.

"You two are amazing!" Rachel exclaimed. "Thank goodness you were here!"

With a happy smile, Kirsty fastened the sunflower necklace around Hope's neck.

"Thank you, all of you," said Hope. "Now, let's hurry to the palace before Jack Frost turns up."

Gladly, the fairies rose into the air and turned towards Fairyland. As they

flew away, they saw the trolls stumping back to Troll Hollow. The goblins were firing boulder cakes at them from the battlements.

The further the fairies got from the castle, the happier they felt. Soon, Fairyland was spreading out below them like a patchwork quilt, and the bright sunshine was warming their wings. Rachel and Kirsty pointed out some of their favourite places as they flew.

"There's the Magic Forest in the distance."

"I can see the Sweet Factory!"

"That's the Lemonade Sea, and there's the Silver Sea."

"Those are the Western Woods – some of the boy fairies live on the other side, but we haven't visited there yet . . ."

Gracie and Khadijah turned their heads this way and that, trying to take everything in. They saw sparkling streams, toadstool houses and buttercup meadows, as well as fairies waving to them from every direction. It felt like no time before they were

fluttering down beside the silver palace. The King and Queen were standing outside, and the fairies sank into low curtsies.

"Your Majesties, my magical objects are safe," Hope burst out. "It's all thanks to our human friends."

"Thank you all," said King Oberon.

"Because of you, newcomers will always find a friendly welcome," Queen Titania added. "I am happy to know that Fairyland has you four as friends."

With a tap of her wand, she refilled their lockets. Hope hugged them all.

"Now we must say goodbye," Queen Titania went on. "After all, there is a party waiting for you in the human world. But I hope that you will visit us again soon."

Amid calls of "Goodbye" and "See you soon!" the Queen waved her wand.

Glittering fairy dust swirled around them.

"It's like swimming through stars," Khadijah exclaimed.

Half dazzled, the four friends blinked and found themselves back in Hawthorn Grove. They were still just around the corner from the party.

"It's good to be home," said Gracie.

Not a second had passed in the human world, and yet everything was different. The street party was in full swing. People were making new friends and trying new foods. Some of them were dancing to the music, including Mrs Tate and Khadijah's dad. Hawthorn Grove rang with laughter.

"I see four seats together," cried Kirsty. "Come on!"

It was a wonderful party. There were foil hats and streamers, a feast of dishes from every family and lots of jokes and laughter. After they had eaten, the four friends got up to dance, spinning around until they were dizzy and giggling.

"I'm so glad you both moved here," said Kirsty.

"Yes," Rachel agreed. "Three cheers for your new home."

"And lots of new adventures," added Gracie.

"Moving here was the best decision our families ever made," said Khadijah. "Hip, hip, HURRAY!"

The End

Now it's time for Kirsty and
Rachel to help ...

Niamh the Invitation Fairy

Read on for a sneak peek ...

"I'm stuffed," said Gracie Adebayo, patting her tummy.

"Me too," said Kirsty Tate. "If I have one more bite, I think I'll pop."

"Best barbecue *ever*," said Khadijah Khan, who was sitting beside her on the swinging chair. "Kirsty, your dad makes amazing food."

Kirsty grinned at her new friends. They had just moved to Hawthorn Grove, Wetherbury's new housing estate. Kirsty's parents had invited them and their families to the barbecue.

"Can anyone manage another burger?"

called Mr Tate from across the garden.

Five burgers and ten corn on the cobs were sizzling on the barbecue. A small crowd gathered, including Khadijah's older brother, Rafi.

"Rafi loves barbecues," said Khadijah, grinning at her brother.

Rafi grinned back at her and rubbed his belly to make her laugh.

"What does Rafi have on his arm?" asked Kirsty.

"It's a special type of pump," said Khadijah. "He has a disease called diabetes. The pump gives him his medicine at the right time each day."

Mr Tate happily snapped his barbecue tongs.

"My dad loves barbecues too," said Kirsty, laughing.

She gazed around the garden and smiled. The setting sun was lending everything in the garden a glimmer of gold. It made her think of the magical glow that was a sign that a fairy adventure would soon begin.

Kirsty and her best friend, Rachel Walker, had been friends with the fairies ever since they had first met on Rainspell Island. During an adventure with Hope the Welcome Fairy, they had been able to share their special fairy secret with Gracie and Khadijah too.

"What shall we do now?" asked Khadijah. "The grown-ups are just going to stand around all evening talking."

"I was hoping you might help me," said Gracie. "It's my birthday soon, and the party is going to be at Partyland."

"Wow!" gasped Kirsty. "Lucky you!"

"What's Partyland?" asked Khadijah.

"It's an amazing adventure park," said Kirsty. "I've only been once. It's huge. There are lots of different areas with their own themes."

"Like what?" asked Khadijah.

"So many I can't remember them all," Kirsty admitted. "Dinosaurs, unicorns, pirates, fairy tales, circus . . . and lots more. There are fairground rides, games, drop slides, a gigantic soft play castle, cafés, water rides, rollercoasters, a petting zoo . . . I only saw a tiny part of it when I went. It's got the biggest mirror maze in the country."

"It sounds fantastic," said Khadijah.

"You're both invited of course," said Gracie. "I was hoping that you would help me to write my party invitations. I brought them with me. Mum and Mama want me to invite everyone from my new class in school, so I can get to know them before term starts. That's a lot of invitations to write!"

"Of course we'll help," said Kirsty. "We can use my sparkly gel pens."

Soon they were lying on their stomachs in Kirsty's sitting room, working through the pile of invitations. Kirsty was just writing one for Rachel when she heard the letterbox rattle.

"It's too late to be the post," she said, jumping to her feet. "Maybe it's a late barbecue guest."

She went into the hall. The letterbox was flapping open and shut, and a bright golden light was shining through it.

"That's not the evening sun," said Kirsty

under her breath. "That's magic!"

To her delight, a tiny fairy tumbled through the letterbox and landed on the doormat with a bump and a merry laugh.

"Oh dear," she said. "I keep hoping that I'll learn to be graceful, but I'm not so sure! Hello, Kirsty. I'm Niamh the Invitation Fairy."

Kirsty thought that no one could help loving Niamh's warm smile. She had ginger hair braided into two thick plaits, green glasses and a dusting of freckles on her cheeks. Her purple T-shirt sparkled with gold stars, and she was wearing a pair of denim dungarees with purple and white starry shoes.

"I'm so glad to meet you," Kirsty said. "Gracie, Khadijah, come out here. There's someone I'd like you to meet."

Gracie and Khadijah dashed into the hall and gasped.

"This is Niamh the Invitation Fairy," Kirsty explained.

"It's lovely to meet you all," said Niamh, fluttering into the air. "I'm here to give each of you a very special invitation."

She waved her wand, and three envelopes appeared in front of the girls. There was a peach one for Gracie, a green one for Khadijah and a pink one for Kirsty. Each was sealed with a colourful star sticker.

"I'm one of the Birthday Party Fairies," Niamh went on. "It's our job to help Belle the Birthday Fairy to create perfect birthday parties, and we've been busy getting ready for the most important birthday of the year. We'd love you to be there to help us celebrate."

The girls quickly opened their envelopes. The invitations were printed on lilac card, with engraved gold lettering.

The Birthday Fairies
are pleased to invite
YOU!
to Queen Titania's royal birthday party
in the garden of Fairyland Palace
this Saturday at 2pm.

Kirsty's heart skipped a beat.

"Oh, thank you!" she said, gazing at the invitation in delight. "We'd love to come, wouldn't we, girls?"

"A party in Fairyland?" said Gracie in a whisper. "Amazing!"

"It's going to be the best party ever," said

Niamh, beaming. "We've planned bubbles and ice cream, fairground rides, a bouncy castle, a pool party and so many other things that it would take me all night to tell you. It's really special because she only celebrates her birthday with a big party every twenty years."

"It sounds wonderful," said Khadijah. "I can't wait!"

There was a sudden crash from the sitting room. The girls ran back in with Niamh fluttering behind them, and their happiness changed to alarm. Two goblins were rifling through Gracie's invitations!

"Let's just copy the words," said the taller goblin. "Quickly, before those pesky humans come back."

"No," the other goblin snapped. "This Partyland place is supposed to be the best.

We have to go there and make sure we copy the best. There are bound to be loads of invitations there."

"I don't want to," the taller goblin whinged. "I'm tired. I just want to go home and eat bogmallows."

"Jack Frost will turn you *into* a bogmallow if we don't get this right," the other goblin warned, scrunching his hands into fists. "Not to mention Jilly Chilly."

Kirsty noticed that one of his fists was holding something rainbow-coloured. It was strange to see a goblin with something so pretty.

"Who's Jilly Chilly?" asked Gracie.

Her voice made the goblins whirl around.

"Run!" shouted the tallest one.

They raced to the open window, jumped out and sprinted down the street. Kirsty ran to the window just in time to see them turning the corner at the end of the road.

"Did they take any of your invitations?" asked Niamh, fluttering down on to Gracie's little arm.

Gracie shook her head.

"What were they doing here?" Khadijah asked.

"I don't know," said Kirsty, feeling anxious. "It's never a good sign when we hear Jilly Chilly's name. She's Jack Frost's sister, and she's just as mean as he is."

"Double trouble," Niamh agreed.

The pile of invitations on the floor suddenly rustled. Khadijah jumped back in shock. Then there was a flurry of sparkles, and three tiny fairies popped out.

"What are you all doing here?" exclaimed Niamh, smiling. "Girls, these are my fellow

Birthday Party Fairies: Sara the Party Games Fairy, Lois the Balloon Fairy and Leahann the Birthday Present Fairy."

It was clear the fairies were very upset. Sara was trembling, Lois had tears running down her face and Leahann was trying to comfort her.

"What's wrong?" Kirsty asked, dropping to her knees so that she could get closer to them.

"It's Jack Frost," said Sara in a shaky voice. "He is trying to destroy Fairyland, once and for all."

"But how?" asked Niamh.

Leahann looked up from rubbing Lois's back. She was very pale.

"He has stolen our precious birthday charms," she said. "He burst in to our party planning workshop after you left,

Niamh. He took everything: your rainbow invitation, my party hat, Lois's balloons and Leahann's present."

"Did he say why?" asked Kirsty urgently. "If we can understand what he wants, we can make a plan to stop him."

Lois looked up, her face streaked with silvery tears.

"He wants to stop Queen Titania and King Oberon being in charge," she said. "He said that he is going to rule alongside Jilly Chilly. They will be the Ice King and Queen."

"He can't do that," cried Khadijah. "He just can't!"

"He can, now that he has our charms," said Sara. "You see, he is going to make Jilly Chilly's official royal birthday the same day as Queen Titania's birthday."

"But how can *that* make Jilly Chilly the queen?" asked Gracie.

"The birthday party is created with our magic," said Niamh. "There is a ceremony during the party that renews Queen Titania's right to be queen for the next twenty years. It's an official ceremony under Fairyland law. Jilly Chilly could use our magic to take the right to be queen!"

Sara waved her wand, and a picture flickered on the mirror over the mantelpiece. Kirsty shivered when she saw the bony figure of Jack Frost. His white hair and beard were stiff with icicles, and frost crackled at the edges of the mirror.

"All of Fairyland will see that Jilly Chilly and I hold the real power," he hissed. "I shall order my goblins to change the words on the invitations. The guests will come to my Ice Castle for the party, and the ceremony will give my sister the right to be queen – *by law!*"

Read Niamh the Invitation Fairy to find out what adventures are in store for Kirsty and Rachel!

Meet Gracie and Khadijah, Fairyland's newest friends!

Read about their magical adventures
in all new Rainbow Magic books!

Meet the Birthday Party Fairies.
Without their celebratory magic,
birthday parties everywhere are ruined.

Find out how Rachel, Kirsty, Gracie and
Khadijah help the fairies to throw Queen
Titania the best birthday party ever in these
stories.

Calling all parents, carers and teachers!

The Rainbow Magic fairies are here to help your child enter the magical world of reading. Whatever reading stage they are at, there's a Rainbow Magic book for everyone! Here is Lydia the Reading Fairy's guide to supporting your child's journey at all levels.

Starting Out

Our Rainbow Magic Beginner Readers are perfect for first-time readers who are just beginning to develop reading skills and confidence. Approved by teachers, they contain a full range of educational levelling, as well as lively full-colour illustrations.

1

Developing Readers

Rainbow Magic Early Readers contain longer stories and wider vocabulary for building stamina and growing confidence. These are adaptations of our most popular Rainbow Magic stories, specially developed for younger readers in conjunction with an Early Years reading consultant, with full-colour illustrations.

2

Going Solo

The Rainbow Magic chapter books – a mixture of series and one-off specials – contain accessible writing to encourage your child to venture into reading independently. These highly collectible and much-loved magical stories inspire a love of reading to last a lifetime.

3

www.orchardseriesbooks.co.uk

"Rainbow Magic got my daughter reading chapter books. Great sparkly covers, cute fairies and traditional stories full of magic that she found impossible to put down" – Mother of Edie (6 years)

"Florence LOVES the Rainbow Magic books. She really enjoys reading now" – Mother of Florence (6 years)

Read along the Reading Rainbow!

Well done - you have completed the book!

This book was worth 2 stars

See how far you have climbed on the Reading Rainbow opposite.
The more books you read, the more stars you can colour in
and the closer you will be to becoming a Royal Fairy!

Do you want to print your own Reading Rainbow?

1. Go to the Rainbow Magic website
2. Download and print out the poster
3. Colour in a star for every book you finish and climb the Reading Rainbow
4. For every step up the rainbow, you can download your very own certificate.

There's all this and lots more at
orchardseriesbooks.co.uk

You'll find activities, stories, a special newsletter AND you can
search for the fairy with your name!